I0734456

MARY CRAWFORD

If You Knew Me

...AND OTHER SILENT MUSINGS

HIDDEN BEAUTY NOVELLA 1

COPYRIGHT

Published on November 2, 2016, by Mary Crawford. The author can be reached at Mary@MaryCrawford.com

ISBN: 978-1-945637-53-7

Cover by Covers Unbound

Hidden Beauty Series

Until the Stars Fall from the Sky

So the Heart Can Dance

Joy and Tiers

Love Naturally

Love Seasoned

Love Claimed

If You Knew Me (and other silent musings) (novella)

Jude's Song

The Price of Freedom (novella)

Paths Not Taken

Dreams Change (novella)

Heart Wish

Tempting Fate

The Letter

The Power of Will

Hidden Hearts Series

Identity of the Heart

Sheltered Hearts

Hearts of Jade

Port in the Storm (novella)

Love is More Than Skin Deep

Tough

Rectify

Pieces (a crossover novel)

Hearts Set Free

Freedom (a crossover novel)

The Long Road to Love (novella)

Love and Injustice (Protection Unit)

Out of Thin Air (Protection Unit)

Soul Scars (Protection Unit)

OTHER WORKS:

The Power of Dictation

Use Your Voice

Vision of the Heart

#AmWriting: A Collection of Letters to Benefit The Wayne Foundation

DEDICATION

For the friends who see us

as we really are

and who we hope to be.

The ones who are by our side as

we fight against those who see

only ugliness in the world

and those who try to

make us feel small.

We breathe easier because of your presence in our lives.

Chapter One

Sadie

Looking around cautiously, I'm a little disappointed. This is nothing like I expected it to be. I guess I had built it up in my head to be a magical place — unlike anything I'd ever been to or experienced before. Aside from the fact it's overwhelmingly loud, this high school is just like every School for the Deaf I've ever attended since preschool. Girls still shriek, hug each other like it's an Olympic sport, wear too much makeup, smell like they've bathed in perfume, and laugh like every joke is the funniest thing they've ever heard.

The difference is, with my cochlear implants, I can now hear all of this chaos. My parents are super protective and didn't want me to leave my little cocoon. So, this is the first time I've been able to venture out of the safety of the deaf community. I'm not really sure whether to be scared or excited. "Normal" high school doesn't seem all that special.

My grades are top-notch. They always have been. I pay meticulous attention to them. I don't want anyone judging my worth by my inability to hear. Honestly, it's a sore spot for me. I always hated it when people call me retarded because of nerve damage. "The tragedy" was so stupid too — when I was a kid, my dad was rear-ended by some idiot, and nobody knew I was severely injured because everything seemed fine on the surface. It wasn't until I stopped responding to people that they figured out there was a problem.

My parents are worried I won't be able to compete on the "big kids' stage." I think they forget I started solving algebra problems in the second grade because I was bored.

I'm a little nervous about being able to fit in here. I don't really have any friends. There's a guy who transferred from my old school just a couple years ago, but I think he's a senior. He probably won't want anything to do with me because I'm a freshman. So, I'm going to stick out as a loner. Girls are weird that way. They judge you by the friends you hang out with, and since I don't actually have any, I'll be at a disadvantage. My plan of attack is to simply pretend to be as normal as humanly possible.

It was weird trying to guess what people would be wearing today. Most of the time, I don't think about it much. I just wear whatever I want to. My mom wants me to dress like a mini businessperson because she says it projects an image of success to my teachers and everyone around me. I'm more prone to wear yoga pants or a bodysuit with a big old sweater over it, but whatever.

I'm still fighting with the combination lock on my locker when something catches my eye. There's a very large mob of people coming my way, and they don't seem to see me. I start to sign, *"Hey! Watch where you're going."* About four beats too late, I remember that I need to use my voice.

A guy so tall he probably plays on the basketball team, sneers at me as he comments to his friends in a singsong voice, "Look, Elijah, they found you another retard to play with at recess."

Another kid pipes up, "Yeah, Defuct-o-matic, maybe you should get together with this one and make a bunch of little freaks."

Crap. I haven't even been here ten minutes, and they're already calling me names. Why did I think this was such a good idea again?

At first, it's not even clear who they're talking about. The scene is so jumbled and chaotic, I'm having trouble figuring out what's going on. People stream through the hallway. A bunch of the kids don't even seem to notice I'm there and they smash me against my locker. I stuff my backpack behind me so it doesn't get stolen in the commotion.

Suddenly, I hear a booming voice from down the hall. It's so loud, I probably could've heard it without my implants. "Is there a problem here?"

"No, Mr. King … no problem … just going to class." The tall kid scurries away.

The man looks at me. "Ms. Anderson, problem?"

Oh just fab, he already knows my name too — so much for being invisible.

"No, sir — I mean yes," I stammer. "I can't seem to get this stupid combination lock to work."

"Why don't you try for a few more minutes? If you still can't get it open, I'll have the janitorial crew give you a hand — just stop by the office. Tell them Vice-Principal King gave you permission to be in the hall."

"Yes, sir," I mumble.

He looks at his watch and hits his forehead. "I'm sorry, Sadie. I can't believe I forgot the conference call with the school board. I have to run."

I stand by my locker and ponder the last few minutes in complete shock. I wonder how I'm going to explain to my parents that the vice principal of the school is already on a first name basis with me when I haven't even been to class yet.

I notice the crowd has dispersed, leaving a pale, shaky kid who's currently so busy trying to stem the trickle of blood from his nose that he apparently doesn't notice my presence. Geez, what do I do now? Should I get the principal? Mr. King seemed to overlook the guy, but he said he would be in a meeting, so I don't even know if he can help me. Maybe the guy doesn't want me to call a teacher anyway.

Since I haven't been able to unpack the truckload of extra crap my mom stuffed in my backpack this morning, I'm able to retrieve the box of Kleenex she insisted I bring to keep in my locker. My mom still thinks I need to do an annual school supply run, as if I'm a kindergartener picking out my first set of jumbo crayons.

Quietly, I walk up to the guy and tap him on the shoulder before wordlessly offering him my box of tissues. He punches wildly and almost knocks them out of my hand. Instinctively, I duck.

He blinks rapidly and slaps the side of his face as if he can't stop it. Finally, he takes a deep breath and looks at me. Slowly, it dawns on him that I'm not with the same group of kids who beat him up. "Jigger … sorry … jig … jigger —"

Usually, context helps me figure this stuff out. I still rely on lip-reading, even though I have the implants — but this just isn't making *any* sense. What I think it sounds like doesn't even remotely apply to me. I must have misheard. Maybe I'm getting some odd feedback or something. Whoever this guy is, he doesn't look like he'd be in a position to mess with me. If I thought my day was off to a rough start, his is far worse.

I pull a Kleenex from the box and stuff it into his hand, "This will help. Hold some pressure on your nose."

"Jig, jigger if you want to survive in this school jig jigger, you should pretend jigger you don't know me … and I need to act like I don't know you. Thanks for the help though."

Chapter Two

Elijah

WELL, THAT'S JUST GREAT. So much for my dad's lectures all summer about how this would be a fresh start for me —about how everyone was going to have a new level of maturity. *It will be different,* they said. *You all are high schoolers now. Kids know more now because of the Internet. They'll understand Tourette's syndrome. They'll know you're smart and that your tics are just a difference like everything else.*

Yeah, not so much. It's been this way ever since Scotty McDougall decided to make Cub Scout camp all about torturing me. From that moment on, Elijah Fischer became synonymous with wimp, target, weirdo, retard, stupid, reject, and my favorite of all, Defuct-o-matic or maybe Jigger-nut because of my tic. I thought the new medication I tried over the summer was doing a pretty good job of controlling my tics, but I guess I was wrong. *Again.* What else is new?

Really? Did I have to fall to pieces in front of one of the prettiest girls I've seen in forever? I had one chance to make a good first impression, and I practically biffed her in the face. I look down at my shirt and see a growing spot of red. Great! This was a brand-new shirt I recently got at an Aidan O'Brien concert. It even has his autograph on the back. I'll never get the blood out.

I walk to my first period class — of course, because I'm late, there are no seats in the back. The only seat in the room is right next to the new girl. I try to slide into my seat before the teacher notices. Just my luck, it's somebody new. "Mr. Fischer, I presume?"

I nod tightly, and inexplicably, New Girl smiles at me and waves.

The new teacher gives me a look of sympathy, a hair shy of pity. "Mondays are tough on me, too. I have an extra copy of the syllabus and handouts for you."

As the teacher cheerfully tells us about her attendance policy and all the exciting things we will do in her class this year, New Girl slips me a note. I honestly don't know how to react. I don't have a great history with notes. Usually, they involve threats to bodily parts I'd rather not lose. I open this one with extreme trepidation. Surprisingly, it just has a few random doodles on it. Okay, so it's not fair to call them doodles — they're pretty much works of art. Among all the doodles is a note:

Her handwriting is almost a work of art in itself. I blink just to make sure I'm not seeing things.

Hi, are you okay?
   I'm Sadie.
   Not to be Capt. Obvious, but I new.
   I'm deaf. Texting or notes are great.
I have a CI so I can hear you. But, it's hard in the hallways because it's crazy. I hope the rest of your year goes better.
~ SA

I tear off a piece of paper from my tablet and scribble.

   Sadie,

   Seriously, if you value your social life here, you need to hate me.

   Trust me. It'll be easier for everybody.

   — Elijah

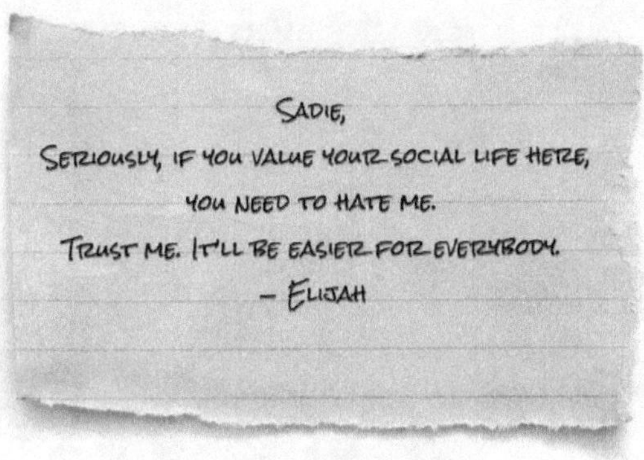

After looking at Sadie's note, I wish my handwriting was better. Usually, I'm in such a rush to get my ideas down that I don't take the time to pay attention to my writing. If I do focus on my writing, I can get too engrossed and repetitively count the strokes in the letters, and that's bad. It's easier for me to rush through and not get distracted by the actual physical act of writing. I'm just weird that way. I carefully fold the note up and pass it to her.

She rolls her eyes while she reads my note. I cringe because I'm afraid the teacher will catch on to her body language if she's not careful. Sadie seems completely oblivious as she hurriedly scribbles an answer. I've never seen anybody write as fast as she does.

In no time flat, a note appears on my desk. As if the speed writing wasn't impressive enough, there's a whole new doodle. It's astonishingly accurate for the amount of time she had to draw it.

I can't believe she had enough time to write that whole thing in what seemed like a few seconds. I wonder if she's talking about the rumor about Kaylynn. She supposedly tried the stupid cinnamon trick and almost died from an asthma attack. She and her friends were trying to make a viral video. It almost went viral for all the wrong reasons.

I read the note slowly again to make sure I didn't miss anything.

I refuse to have a bunch of people who are dumb enough to believe that what they see on the Kardashians has anything to do with real life, who measure their social worth by whether they can hold a pen under their boobs, get free from duct tape or set themselves on fire with Axe, decide who my friends can or can't be. If you're cool with me, I'm cool with you. Deal?
 ~ SA
She takes a second to write down something the teacher says.

To be honest, I don't think I've heard more than about four words of what's been said in class for the last forty minutes. I try again to dissuade her with another note.

Sadie,

I still don't think any of this is a good idea.

I have dealt with these people since I was in kindergarten. They are vicious. We need to stay away from each other. The stakes are bigger than online pranks.

— EF

I surreptitiously watch for her reaction from behind my binder. She rolls her eyes at me and presses her lips together in frustration. Subtlety is not her strong point. The new teacher starts to talk about her grading policies, and I try to pay attention for a change, but it's just no use.

I'm totally distracted by everything going on this morning. Suddenly, a new note appears on the edge of my desk.

I feel like the universe is punking me when I allow her words to sink in.

It's too late now. You and I have been matched as study-buddies. It'll be hard to pretend we don't know each other.
What time would you like to study...
Partner?
~SA

CHAPTER THREE

SADIE

MAYBE I WAS A little overconfident in my ability to combat the social forces of the entire school. For the third time this week, the clothes in my locker after fourth period PE class are completely drenched with soda. Right now, I'm hating my decision to leave my comfort zone and go to public school with mainstreamed kids.

My parents think regular classes are an asinine idea — there's a SAT vocab word for you. For once, they might be right. Yet, trying to go to the best college is actually the driving force behind this insane experiment that is my life. I don't want my first experience navigating the hearing world in an academic environment to be the day I step foot on my college campus.

Speaking of college campuses, today was supposed to be the day for me — the day I would get to actually speak to someone about my dreams. Not the dreams my parents have for me, but *my* dreams. Now, I may not get my chance because of some crazy, power-hungry, backstabbers. Of course, they don't care about that. I busted my butt to get special permission to go to this presentation. They usually only let juniors and seniors attend. Representatives from the art departments of Carnegie Mellon, Columbia University, and Virginia Commonwealth University will be there. I still can't believe they came all the way out to Oregon.

Unfortunately, I can't go dressed like this. Furious at myself and my stupid circumstances, I wipe tears from my face as I toss my clothes in the garbage. I always hated this outfit my mom makes me wear anyway. It makes me look about forty-five years old.

I'm so far ahead in math class that it's not even funny, so I send my math teacher a text and tell him I have a headache.

I walk outside and sit down beside my favorite tree. I know it's weird to have a favorite tree, but I do. It's got the perfect root structure to lean against while you're reading a book or drawing. I close my eyes and let the September sun warm my body.

It isn't long before I hear Elijah coming; It isn't hard to distinguish him from other people. We've had plenty of time to get to know each other. Except for math and science, we have identical schedules and we hang out a lot.

I've learned enough about him to know something must have really upset him, because I can hear him muttering his tic all the way across the yard. He's become comfortable enough around me, he generally tells me if he feels a flurry of them coming on. Apparently, if he consciously tries to hold them back, it makes them worse.

"Jigger, jigger, jigger jig, jigger, what are you doing?" he asks me, after gaining his composure.

I worry so much about him when he's ticcing this much because he involuntarily hits his face. It seems like it must hurt, but he says he doesn't even notice.

"Rough day in PE. I don't want to talk about it." My speech sounds off — even to me. I usually try to disguise the distortions in my speech as much as I can, but when I'm distraught or extremely fatigued, they leak through.

"I heard. It's all over school. In fact, it's probably all over jigger, jigger, jigger jig, jigger Facebook, YouTube, Snapchat, and Twitter by now. I'm sorry. I tried to warn you. These idiots won't stop until they completely destroy you. Jigger, jigger, jigger jig, jigger … It's been their mission in my life for almost a decade. This was my battle to fight. I shouldn't have dragged you into the middle of this."

"Elijah, I hate to burst your bubble. You don't get to choose my battles. *I* choose them and *you* are worth fighting for."

"How do you know I'm worth fighting for?" Elijah grimaces. Without warning, his hands claw at the side of his neck and face. His verbal tic is so bad, he can barely get any words out.

I know I can't do anything to stop his tics, but I hop up and try to pull his sweatshirt sleeves down over his hands so his nails don't cut his face or hurt his eyes.

His eyes are wide with fear as I come closer. "Jigger, jigger, Sadie, jigger jig jigger, *stop!* I don't want to hurt you."

I manage to pull his sleeves over his hands as I answer him softly. "I know you don't. I don't want you to hurt yourself either, which is why I have to help. I know the risks."

"Jigger, jigger. It's too much risk. Jigger, jig, jig."

"So is standing by, doing nothing." I use the bottom of my oversize basketball jersey to wipe some blood off his forearm.

"Don't you have a thing to go to during lunch?" he asks, suddenly focusing on my workout gear.

"Yeah, but my clothes are ruined, and my parents are both out of town today," I explain bitterly.

"Jig-jigger, lucky for you, my sister, Mariam, left a bunch behind when she went to college. You look about the same size. I only live four houses down. *Mi casa es su casa...*"

———•———

I got permission from my art teacher to stay after school and paint some pictures for my portfolio because the recruiters from the college programs were so enthusiastic over my work — especially the ones from Carnegie Mellon. I'm relieved Mrs. Connor had to stay after and grade exams because I need to work out some of my frustration over the day.

Elijah is a great friend, but he doesn't need to be all keyed up over my chaotic emotions. It was super cool for him to give his sister's old clothes, but I could tell he was upset my belongings were messed with on such an important day.

I dump all of my negative emotions on the canvas in dark swirls of color. It's been an exhausting day. Finally after I add to several layers of texture, I have to let it dry. I cleanup my brushes and thank Mrs. Connor as I grab my backpack and walk home.

I didn't realize how late it was until my mother confronts me at the door. "Sadie Anderson, why do you look like a homeless person? What happened to the perfectly good suit I purchased you at JCPenney's?"

I drop my heavy book bag on the stairs and lean against the banister. Tears gather at the corner of my eyes. I wish it was the old days and I could pretend I didn't hear my mom and just go upstairs and hide in my room — but I can't. I turn and face her. "It was ruined."

"What do you mean, it was ruined?"

"I guess somebody's hazing me. They…umm …dumped soda on it and burned it with matches or something while I was dressed down for PE."

"What? Did you tell a teacher? See I told you not to go to that school! You have perfectly good friends at the School for the Deaf. I still don't know why you got a wild hair to go to another school. They treated you well at your old school."

"Mom —" I try to interrupt.

"Don't you think you should go back to the School for the Deaf? You have lots of great friends there. No one would've set your clothes on fire there. Maybe you just don't fit in the hearing world."

"Mom, that's not fair! Every new student gets picked on. This might not even have anything to do with my deafness. After all, this is high school. They do things differently in high school. I might have even gotten picked on at the School for the Deaf in high school."

"I keep telling you that you have to carry yourself with confidence. Otherwise, people are going to walk all over you." She wrinkles her nose at me as she examines me up and down. Of course, I've got paint on my face and under my fingernails. "Where in the world did you get those clothes — the lost and found or something?"

"A friend gave them to me, they're his sister's," I mumble.

"Are you still hanging out with that strange kid?" my mom asks. "A lady from my Pilates class told me about him. I guess none of the kids like him. What are you doing hanging out with him? If you want to make friends at your new school, you should be hanging out with the popular kids."

"Mom, that's not even true. He's a very nice guy. I like him. You should be grateful. Because of Elijah, I still got to meet with the admissions people who were at school today. They really liked me. Some of them are even talking scholarship even though I'm only a freshman. The guy from Carnegie Mellon seemed really impressed by me."

My mom perks up. "Carnegie? They have a really good engineering program there. Your math scores are really good."

"They do, but their art program is also phenomenal. The recruiter was really impressed by my portfolio."

She just shakes her head in disgust. "Art? When are you going to grow up and use the brains God gave you? Nobody ever goes anywhere painting pretty pictures. Get real! I knew we never should've let you change schools and get new friends."

I wipe away tears as I pick up my backpack and start to

go upstairs. "Maybe someday you'll trust that I really am smart," I whisper as I climb the stairs and throw my backpack on my bed and collapse on my beanbag chair and dissolve into tears.

What if she's right and I've made all the wrong decisions?

CHAPTER FOUR

ELIJAH

I DON'T OFTEN GET to feel like the hero in the books I read, but I totally do. It was a small thing, but for Sadie, I saved the day. It was beyond epic.

Once Mrs. Gable figured out I knew some sign language from all the time I've spent in "behavioral classrooms" as a kid, she decided Sadie and I are fated partners — as she calls us — so she kept us together, even after the first assignment.

I've known Sadie for a few months now, but I've never seen her so excited. I guess those college recruiters were pretty impressed with her initiative as a freshman and asked to see her portfolio. Understandably, they were pretty blown away. Next term, Sadie and I are going to use our elective class to work on a special project with Mrs. Gable.

Like clockwork, we meet by our tree after class. Sadie has advanced chemistry, and I'm not quite there yet. Her class is in the senior wing of the school, so it takes her a while to get all the way over to this side of the building. I take the time to set up a little picnic area for us. I've started to bring a special backpack just for our afternoon sessions. What can I say? It beats going home alone.

My mom is an investigator who looks at nursing homes to see if they comply with the law. She works really weird hours so she can catch them off guard when they're not expecting an inspection. My dad is an inspector for bridges and highway construction. He's gone most of the week and comes home on the weekends. Then, in the winter or when it's too stormy to work outside, he's home a lot. Since my sister is away at college, I'm pretty much left to fend for myself. If nothing else, this project is a nice distraction from my boring life.

I look up as Sadie runs toward me with a wide grin on her face. It's weird how much one person has changed my life in a little more than a dozen weeks. I used to worry a lot about what other people thought of me, but I'm starting to adopt Sadie's attitude. Something about having her watch my back makes it a little easier for me to hold my head up. It's not as if the creeps have let up any. Sadie has simply made it easier to let it all go.

Sadie's definition of me is so much different from theirs, it almost gives me permission to define myself differently too. Having her as a friend is a powerful thing. I know now at least one person sees me completely differently than Scott and all the classless jerks he calls friends.

"You look happy," I observe. "Did you get an A or something?"

"Better than that!" Sadie says as she dances around in a little circle, "Didn't you hear Mrs. G.? She said we get to publish a book, like real authors on Amazon and everything. How do you think we should sign our names at the book signings?"

"Yeah, I heard her." I hold my hands up in the timeout signal. "Jigger, jig, jig, I don't think you guys understand. I've never really written anything before. I just read books or watch movies I like and cast the characters as if the underdog or the least favorite character was the winner of the fight or gets the girl. Mostly, I just write because I'm bored. I don't think anybody would ever pay attention to what I write. What makes her think someone would take my ideas seriously?"

Sadie digs in my backpack and throws me a candy bar. "Eat something. You're getting 'hangry'." She shakes her head at me as she continues. "Maybe she thinks you're extremely talented because … I don't know … perhaps she reads your papers like, every other day and grades them against two or three hundred other English students."

I narrow my gaze at her. "Exaggerate much?"

She shrugs slightly as she admits, "Maybe a little, but not much. You consistently do better on your papers than I do, and not many people have that distinction. For eight years of my academic career, no one has ever smoked me before you. Fischer, I think we can do this. In fact, I think our pen name should be Anderson Fischer. It's a great name, don't you think?"

"Okay, let's say I buy your premise, jigger, jig, jig … and your nom de plume? What in the world do we make this story about? We're in high school. We don't have a lot of experience. I've never even had a girlfriend. Have you had a boyfriend?"

Sadie laughs. "With my overprotective parents? Forget

about it. I used to have a wicked crush on Aidan O'Brien — but I got to meet his wife before they even got engaged, and it turns out that I have a pretty big girl crush on her." Sadie blushes and tightens her ponytail holder. "She's a legit artist too. I was there when they got engaged. It was really awesome. I painted her face that night. You want to see? The picture is in my portfolio."

"Hold up!" I practically shout as I do a double take. "You're saying you actually *know* Aidan O'Brien and Tara Isamu. I used her dance videos to storyboard one of my fight scenes, jigger, jig, jig. Have you seen what she does for martial arts? She's like some major dancer, but her tae-kwon-do katas are beyond description. There just aren't words in the English language for her…" I let my speech trail off as I realize I sound like some gushing dweeb.

"I know. I feel the same way when I talk to her," Sadie responds. "It's really weird because she's such a nice person, you forget that she's totally famous. Aidan is the same way. The guy can cuss like a sailor in ASL. It's too funny. He tries not to show his wife, but Tara is a sign language interpreter, so she totally knows. It's like a running joke between the two of them."

My eyes totally bug out. "Jigger, jig, jig, you actually hang with them?"

Sadie giggles. "More than you might think. We actually hang. Aidan has a rock climbing club at their art center."

"Why is this the first time I'm hearing this?" I demand. "How many concert T-shirts do I have? You could've said something! You *know* the dude! Seriously! You know him — like you've eaten off the same silverware?"

Sadie blushes. "It would be super weird for me to name

drop. They're sort of like my friends now. Honestly, it doesn't seem like a big deal anymore. I bet you if we wrote a book, they would help us promote it. You know, Aidan has a cochlear implant like me. He's all about the 'reach for your dream' stuff."

"Yeah, I know. That's why I'm such a big fan — plus his music is totally sweet. I like that he's different, and he doesn't try to hide it, jigger, jig, jig." I drum my fingers nervously before I ask, "Can we go back to the original question? If we write this book, what should we write about?"

"You'll think I'm totally crazy, but I think we should write about high school life and not be obvious about it. I think the whole-reality-TV, Kardashian, TMZ kind of stuff is like the modern-day equivalent of The Emperor's New Clothes. What if we were to do some sort of modern take on the story using current technology–you know, how everybody posts bogus pictures of their life? Girls posting filtered pictures of themselves supposedly wearing no makeup and just rolling out of bed when it's actually taken them three hours to get ready or boys saying they're naturally buff when they're taking steroids. Everybody tries to be the most popular and have the most likes — as if that's even a measurement of true friendship."

I nod. I hate social media. To me it is like a huge locker room on steroids. "Jigger, jig, jig, I don't know which is worse, the real world or the cyber-one." I shudder as I remember my worst encounters.

"It all just seems so fake to me." Sadie stands up and resumes pacing in line in front of me. "I think I have an advantage–when I want to turn off the world, I can. I just turn off my implants and turn the computer off, and the world goes away. I don't know what the rest of you do. Your world can never go away. You always hear the chatter in the background. It must be horribly distracting when you're trying to do your homework."

For a long time, I'm silent as I think about her idea. At first, it seems completely overwhelming to take on all of social media and the way we build our social world. However, thinking about hanging it on the framework of such a simple little story like *The Emperor's New Clothes* is a brilliant idea. I'm immediately intrigued. I can't remember the last time I read it. I think I must've been in kindergarten … maybe. Even so, I feel my writer's Spidey senses start to tingle.

Sadie must be able to tell something is going on. She doesn't even bother to talk to me before she pulls a pad of paper out of my backpack and hands me a pen from hers. Much to my surprise, it's not one of the calligraphy pens she likes to write with and it's not one of mine. It's a nice, heavy, fountain pen. I look up with a puzzled expression.

Sadie gives me a secret smile. "When we become rich and famous, you'll have an awesome story to tell about how your writing partner gave you a special, lucky pen."

"No joke? Jigger, jig, jig, you really think we can do this?" My stomach is tight with fear and anticipation.

"I'm so convinced we can do this, I'm staking my college portfolio on it," she answers with conviction.

"Geez, Sadie! Way to add pressure. You know I don't respond well to stress, jigger, jig, jig," I exclaim, running my hand through my hair.

"I believe you're stronger than you know. We've got

this. We're Anderson Fischer, world-famous author."

Chapter Five

Sadie

When I first transferred to this high school, I thought I would be bored to tears, but this journey is turning out to be completely different from what I expected. I haven't had this much fun since I went to music camp in junior high. Speaking of music, I feel kind of mean, but it's just a little too entertaining to tease Elijah about my friendship with Aidan.

Elijah is far more devious than I ever gave him credit for. He has totally nailed our little microcosm without calling any one person out. The world he's creating with his words is so much fun to actualize in pictures. Even though we have drastically different approaches to our art, we rarely disagree on the outcome. Elijah is getting more excited about the project with each illustration I complete.

It's almost as if he can't fully believe the vast vision he's creating until I show it to him. He doesn't understand that I wouldn't be able to create my illustrations if his words didn't invoke the emotions and feelings while providing incredible details. His characters are so realistic that you want to root for the hero and destroy the villain. The single best part of this is that he's created this whole elaborate world and clever dialogue which has a layer of subtext most people won't recognize as satire about the balance of power issues in modern society.

Elijah has managed to re-create a microcosm of our school in an alternate universe while still loosely re-creating the storyline of *The Emperor's New Clothes*. If I dare mention his epic writing talent, Elijah merely shrugs and acts as if this is something he does all the time.

I can relate. I feel the same way when people talk about my drawing. I've been doodling and spray painting since I can remember. It all started when my dad used to bring me big boxes home from the art department of the graphics design business next door to where he worked.

They used to save me all the half-empty cans from completed projects. I got great at mixing all the colors and making a little tiny bit of paint go a long way. I would make painting masks out of little bits of torn paper and tape and even blades of grass. Little by little, I would use layers of paint to make a complex mural. Soon, neighbors were coming over to see my "masterpieces."

At first, my parents thought my talent was cute. By the time I was nine, my parents were no longer amused. Reluctantly, they bought me real art supplies. Still, they've always made it clear they don't want me to pursue the arts for a living. My mom especially wants me to do something like accounting which requires common sense and logic rather than something ethereal like the arts. I still think even now she believes somehow I'll outgrow my artistic phase.

She had great hopes for me when I cleared the boards with my analytical skills on all my standardized testing. I think she believed if I took enough math classes, I would see that somehow art makes no logical sense, and I would suddenly give up my passion. That's not really the way it works. I'm just one of those very strange people who likes both.

It's amazing how the faculty of the whole school has gotten behind what Elijah and I have called Project Utopia. The theater department is allowing me to use the backstage area to paint all my scenes. I decided to use an airbrush and large canvases to make my initial scenes because that's generally my medium of choice. We're still debating how to best translate the large paintings into actual illustrations for the graphic novel. No one has attempted to do a project like this before, so Ms. Gable's doing some research for me about the most efficient way to get it done.

As I leave to go wash my hands and the airbrush bottles, I remember Mr. Henderson went to the school office to turn in his grades. I prop the door open with a rock as a doorstop.

When I return, I'm horrified to see someone has slashed two of my paintings right down the middle. There's no way this could have been an accident. I don't know who would've even been around. Elijah and I had to get specific permission from the administration and our parents to stay on campus after school, since it's not an organized sports program.

I take inventory of the rest of the paintings and decide it isn't such a great loss, because they didn't destroy my favorites of the group, and I had already taken pictures with my cell phone to show Elijah. I guess this is where my background as a street artist helps. I'm really fast, and I'm used to my work being destroyed. It still stings though. I don't understand why someone would strike out at something so close to me.

Speaking of Elijah, this conversation won't go well. This little development will put me behind and throw him out of his headspace. There's no way I can disguise what I was working on, because we were talking about my pieces this morning. I have to tell him eventually. Elijah gets far more upset when people go after me than he does if they attack him and there's no way to sugarcoat this. This was definitely personal.

I stop by the vending machine in the teachers' lounge, and I'm relieved to see regular junk food. Sometimes there are excellent perks to being a straight A student. There's no doubt about it; this conversation will require a two-pronged approach: sugar and caffeine.

Chapter Six

Elijah

I take the can of Red Bull and the Three Musketeers bar out of Sadie's hands as I ask skeptically, "What happened?"

She looks a little sheepish. "What makes you think something is wrong?"

"Maybe because you've spent most of the past school year telling me this stuff will kill me, so the fact that you're actually trying to get me to eat it means something's up. So, what's going on?"

She unclips her phone from her backpack and scrolls through the pictures, showing me the latest series she just took. "This is what my work looked like about an hour ago, but it doesn't look like that now."

A knot forms in my stomach. "What's changed?"

"If I had to guess, I'd say the Not-So-Silent, Not-The-Majority got to it while I was cleaning my airbrush."

I abruptly jump to my feet. "Jigger, jigger, jigger jig, jigger, I've had *enough*. They can't get away with this. Jigger, jigger, jigger jig, jigger, obviously, the school doesn't care. That group of bullies has been torturing me for years. You've been a target ever since you walked through the doors of this school because you are friends with me. I've got to do something." I stop and shake out my arms, trying to break the tic. "I've been teaching myself martial arts over the Internet for a while now. Jigger, jigger, jigger jig, jigger, maybe it's time for me to put those skills to use, jigger, jigger, jigger jig, jigger."

Sadie does what she's learned to do when I'm ticcing. She walks up behind me and places her arms around me from behind and gives me a hug, laying her head on my shoulder blade. There's something about the fact that she can hear my heart racing which seems to calm me down a bit. Even my parents are reluctant to get very close when I'm in full on Jigger-nut mode, as the other kids call it, but it doesn't even seem to faze Sadie.

Through the sound of my own pulse racing in my eardrum, I hear her say, "I've learned a lot from Tara about facing down bullies, and I don't think she would agree with using martial arts that way. I have a better idea, anyway."

"Jigger, jig, jig, yeah? What are you planning to do, give everyone a smack down yourself because you've studied with the great Tara Isamu?" I snap.

Sadie shakes her head against my back before she lets go of me, sits down by the tree, and pulls me down beside her. She grabs the candy bar from the ground where I dropped it, opens it, and feeds me a bite. "No, we're going to beat them at their own game. We'll just make the

Utopian Fine Arts Society the place to see and be seen. Are you ready? We're about to go from the most unpopular kids in school to the most popular."

I pick up the energy drink and show it to her. "Exactly how many of these have you had? Are you aware that they have a whole wall in the boys' bathroom dedicated to writing insults about me, jigger, jig, jig?"

"So? Now Anderson Fischer is going to have a fan page like none other. What are you doing on Saturday?"

"Nothing much, jigger, jig, jig. My dad says I have to mow the lawn, and I've got a paper due in biology on Monday. Other than that, I was just planning to play a few video games. Why?"

"Heads up, we're launching the Utopian Fine Arts Society at noon on Saturday. Bring a new sharpie. Anderson Fischer is about to go viral in the real world. We are about to change reality. Are you ready?"

"I have absolutely no idea, jigger, jig, jig," I admit.

"I don't think any of us have a clue. That's what this whole project is about, but it will be fun to watch the world change around us." She opens a Three Musketeers bar and takes a bite. "I have a feeling things are about to rock our world," she adds with a grin.

Chapter Seven

Sadie

The thing I love about Tara and Aidan and all of their friends is that they totally support letting it all hang out just to follow your dream. That's what Joy and Tiers is all about. Tara's friend, Heather, is allowing me to take over the patio at her bakery and borrow her social media page for the launch of the Utopian Fine Arts Society. Did I mention she made some kickin' *hors d'oeuvres* and yummy desserts as if this was a huge Hollywood premiere?

A tall kid comes up to me, carrying a tablet and jamming his stylus into his curly hair. He has paint under his fingernails too, but I don't recognize him from my school. He doesn't look old enough to go to college, but you never know these days.

"Hi, I'm Gabriel. I go to West Central, but I play basketball against you guys. Tara is kind of my honorary aunt, and she told me what you guys are doing. I'm all in because your point guard is a jerk. I can't stand guys like him. You wouldn't believe what he called me on the court. I don't know what he has against people who are different, but the guy needs an attitude adjustment. It's too bad the ref didn't hear him, because he would've gotten a technical." Gabriel rolls his eyes in disgust.

Gabriel's really cute, but I guess not everybody appreciates variety.

"That's why we're here. I can't believe so many people pitched in to help." I look at the huge production around me. "I was just planning to draw a few little pictures."

"Yeah, you should probably know that this group does nothing small. Do you want to see what I drew?"

"I should probably show Elijah too," I vacillate as Gabriel gets closer.

"*Okay,*" he signs. "*I'll find my cousin, Mindy. She's probably talking his ear off. She has a thing about books.*"

"*You sign?*" I ask, my jaw slack with astonishment.

He shrugs as he signs, "*Uncle Aidan.*"

"*Name sign, yours?*" I sign back, suddenly nervous.

Just when I thought I couldn't be any more surprised, he shows me a name sign almost identical to mine. The only difference is he uses a G in place of the S on the artist palette.

I smile shyly as I sign, "*Hi, I'm Sadie — name sign same, except with an S.*" Finding my voice, I add, "But you can talk. I have implants."

"Great. You're an artist — you'll probably understand what I did here. I do mostly Anime and comic book stuff. A lot of my work is on the computer. I turned your image into an avatar, but I worked a lot of Elijah's features in there too — like his eye color and his glasses — to make Anderson Fischer. If you guys like it, I can go live with it, and I can put it out to the same demographics as Uncle Aidan's fan base and also my comic book readers on Wattpad. I don't have huge readership compared to his music fans, but it's something, I guess," he trails off with a shrug.

I'm so speechless, I don't even realize Elijah and a tall, willowy blonde girl with riotous curls have come up behind me.

"See? What did I tell you? Cousin Gabriel has all this handled. He's a total marketing genius. Wait until you see what he drew. It's like a clone of you and Sadie," Mindy explains excitedly to Elijah.

I'm startled when she uses my name, but then I take a closer look. "Mindy? Last time I saw you, you were in the fourth grade. When did you get so tall?"

"It was fifth, but my dad says it's because I'm so precocious — my personality has nowhere to go but up," Mindy answers with a laugh.

Gabriel pulls up a mock website and shows it to Elijah and me. It's better than anything I envisioned in my head. I look older and sophisticated — like a real author. It's weird because I'm a cartoon.

Elijah whistles through his teeth. "Wow, Anderson. I had no idea you were hot."

"I'm not," I say. "This is just a figment of our imagination, remember? It's not actually me."

"Something tells me we're going to find that a little harder to remember, the longer this goes on." Elijah shakes his head as he reads the press release about Anderson Fischer's impressive upcoming new release and surprise-

If You Knew Me (and other silent musings)

by-invitation-only media event.

CHAPTER EIGHT

ELIJAH

I have no idea exactly when this spun out of control. Sadie wasn't kidding when she told me to buckle my seatbelt and get ready for a wild ride. It's like something you see on TV. This cannot be my life. There are people lined up outside the store, and they're not here to get cookies — although, the cookies are amazing.

The scheme Sadie dreamed up is sheer genius, but I don't know if she'll be able to pull it off. She assures me she can, and I believe her — I think.

Sadie is drawing little caricatures of each ticket holder– demonstrating to each person her artistic talent. In turn, I'm making a clever satirical comment about their personality by either giving them a sweet little nick-name or one with a few barbs on the tear-off part of the picture, giving them a "coupon" which entitles them to a private pre-release of Anderson Fischer's new novel, being presented by Aidan O'Brien.

Sadie provides Mindy a list of people who have been supportive of us and another of those who haven't, and Mindy and Gabriel are busy sifting through the crowd, shuffling people from one line to another until we get the crowd prioritized, and the first two hundred and fifty people have been given admittance tickets. When Sadie's hand cramps from drawing portraits, much to my shock, Tara shows up and draws right beside her. It's not very often that someone you know from YouTube appears right in front of you, but there she is, helping us out.

⬥

If you would've told me when I was getting the crap beat out of me nearly every day, that one single day would have changed my entire academic career, I would've laughed in your face. Yet, it seems as if Sadie may have pulled it off. Even two months later, people are still treating us with a whole new level of respect. Quite frankly, it's weirding me out a little. I mean, I've always heard it's who you know that makes a difference, but really? This is extreme. We've gone from being the pariahs at school to the people everybody wants to know because we held an event where Aidan O'Brien's wife was present? It doesn't make a lot of sense to me, but I guess I'll enjoy it while it lasts.

What if the book is a flop? Everybody promises me it's not, but it's hard to believe them. I'm trying some new mapping software to better understand how to describe the new utopian world in more precise detail. It's almost impossible to describe what you can't physically see except in your head. Though, Sadie says I'm doing better than great because she's able to translate my words into these breathtaking pictures. Seeing her turn the vision in my head into something so much better is probably the most shocking part of the process to me. I wasn't even sure it was possible. Maybe I'm struggling with it because what I thought was the definition of utopia a few months ago is changing.

Popularity isn't what I thought it was when I didn't have it. I thought everything would be automatically easier if I was popular, but it turns out a few things are harder. When I didn't have any friends except Sadie, it was easy to sort out how people felt about me. Now, whenever somebody tries to have a conversation, I have to figure out what their agenda is, because people who were never nice before, suddenly are going out of their way to talk and try to hang out with me. Some people have genuinely apologized for their behavior and said they only went along with the crowd because they felt like they had too much to lose if they didn't.

Honestly, I don't know how I feel about that. When Sadie first came to school, I told her to be someone fake to get along. If I don't forgive other people for doing the same thing, I'm a huge hypocrite.

Cody Davis slides into the seat next to me and sets his book bag down. "You mind?"

Actually I do, but that's never bothered these guys before.

I casually move my drink over, shrug nonchalantly, and try to control my tic, which always gives me away.

Cody takes a long time to take his books out of his backpack and arrange his notebook and textbooks in front of him. I have no idea what's going on, so I don't have any choice but to sit quietly and wait. I'm worried I won't be able to be quiet much longer, because holding in a tic is kind of like holding your breath underwater. It won't work indefinitely.

I hold my forearm against my mouth as I mumble, "Jigger, jigger, jigger jig, jigger," as quietly as I possibly can against the sleeve of my sweatshirt. I exhale and take a deep drink of water from my water bottle.

Cody clears his throat. "Um … look … I, um, owe you an apology."

"Why?" I narrow my gaze and stare right at him.

"Dude, some respect here. I'm trying to be nice."

"Again, I have to ask why, jigger, jig, jig. Why now? You've been like, Scotty's personal henchman and made it your mission to make my life miserable for as long as I can remember. Why change your mind now? Is it because I might have more popular friends? If that's true, you're pretty lame, because I still have Tourette's, and my best friend is still deaf. I'm still Defuct-o-matic, Jiggernut, and a thousand vile things to you. Jigger, jig, jig, nothing has changed, except you think you might gain something from my friendship."

Cody flushes red as a pained expression crosses his face. He glances nervously around the deserted library. "Can we go somewhere more private?"

I can't help it. I smirk. "Look around. We're not going to get much more private than this, jigger, jig, jig."

"You'd be surprised. Scott has eyes everywhere," Cody says nervously.

I rotate my shoulder and pop it as I twist my back,

"Okay, jigger, jig, jig. I've been sitting here forever anyway. Let's go take a walk."

The whole time I'm gathering up my stuff, I'm trying to puzzle through what he just said. I don't understand where this is going. For as long as I can remember, Cody has been Scotty McMullen's right-hand man — literally. You don't see one of them without the other. I remember one summer when they were hanging around by the town fountain. I was riding my bike to the corner store to get some ice cream. It was a complete tag team deal, like some wrestling move you would see on TV. Cody held my head underwater that time.

Part of me wonders if I'm being set up again. During the time it takes Cody to reassemble his complicated packing system, I text Sadie a cryptic message asking her to swing by and check to see if I'm home in a couple hours and telling her who I'm with — in case something terrible happens to me. I don't trust the current situation. It's too bizarre.

I can't remember the last time anyone from this group of friends had a conversation with me which didn't involve some sort of bodily threat. The fact that he wants to talk to me is so completely baffling, that it borders on straight-up, freak-out-surrealness. If it were anybody except the Prince of the Not-So-Silent, Not-The-Majority Club, I would've probably invited him over to my house. Since I don't know why the heck he wants to even talk to me, I won't take that risk — especially since I can't remember when my parents said they'd be home tonight except that it will be late. Eventually, we end up standing at the base of the tree Sadie and I have started calling our own.

"Okay, you got me out here, jig, jigger. Start talking," I demand.

"You're right. You have every reason to absolutely hate the air I breathe. I wouldn't blame you if you did. You don't trust me. I get it. Listen! You and Sadie did the impossible. You changed the balance of power. For the first time in years, Scotty has lost his grip. People are questioning his popularity. Your fictional character has a bigger following on Twitter and on Instagram than he does — and he's the state champ in sports. He's livid. He doesn't seem to understand that karma bites."

I've heard a lot of people talk about their lives flashing before their eyes under a lot of different scenarios, but this was not one I ever would've considered. It's like a deranged sports highlight reel, all the images since before Cody and I could even tie our shoes appear, and in every single humiliating instance, Cody Mullins plays a starring role. I shake my head in disbelief. "Jigger, jig, jig seriously? You want to talk to me about karma? Jig jigger, jig do I look that stupid to you? I was actually there during those 'little incidents,' remember?"

Cody leans his head back against the tree and scrubs his hand down his face. "I was a jerk. I can't change that. This will sound lame, but I thought I had a good reason until I watched you and Sadie change the rules. It seemed like Scott held all the power with the coaches because his dad is the head coach at the University. Now I'm not sure Scott really matters all that much."

I'm not used to seeing Cody be uncertain. Oddly, I'd thought this moment would be much more satisfying. I actually feel kind of bad for him because this move won't make him popular with the Scotts of the world.

I can hardly believe the words as they come spilling out of my mouth. "Jigger, jig, jig, do you have plans for the Saturday before prom?"

Chapter Nine

Sadie

"IF I EVER TELL you writing a book is fun again, just shoot me." I stretch and flex my fingers. "I swear I've fixed this same typo a dozen times. Are you sure you didn't change the spelling of this character's name?"

"Yes, I'm sure — but I'm not sure if spell check knows, jigger, jig, jig." Elijah chews on the end of a red pencil. "I'm thinking about changing the editing colors. I'm sick of looking at things written in red."

I laugh. "I almost wore a white T-shirt with red and blue stripes this morning, but I looked in the mirror and decided I couldn't handle it — I looked too much like a piece of notebook paper." I stretch my wrists like my keyboarding teacher taught me, but I think I'm beyond preventative exercises now. "Hey, did you know Coach Billings was such a grammar freak? I asked her about it the other day, and she told me that while she was in college, she used to create crossword puzzles for the school newspaper. Her work experience would explain why she's so good at proofreading our stuff—but it doesn't explain why she's working in the PE department and not teaching AP English."

Elijah nods. "You know who else is great? The janitor who works on the senior wing, Mr. Singh, jigger, jig, jig. I guess his middle daughter was an all-star academic on one of those academic competition shows, and he used to help her study all the vocabulary words. Jigger, jig, jig, even though he never graduated from high school, he has a genius level vocabulary."

"That's been one of the weirdest things about writing this book. I thought it would be all about learning things like new words or the craft of building the novel, or as my grandpa would say, the nuts and bolts of it all. I thought we would spend lots of time in the library learning about the methods of writing. I didn't expect to learn about each other and the people we interact with every single day." I shrug as I look through my notes.

"I definitely thought it would be more like a traditional English class. Jigger, jig, jig, I sometimes wonder if there's too much power in our hands," Elijah says. "It's changed the social climate of our school. Doesn't it creep you out a little?"

"Actually, it messes with my head. The other day, Cody fessed up to what he'd done to my paintings. I wasn't going to be a snitch because it wouldn't have fixed anything, but he came clean to the teachers. He was suspended and kicked off the team. I didn't ask him to. I mean, he must've thought there was a good reason to make Scott happy. I can't imagine you would pick on somebody just for the sake of it. Rational, reasonable people don't do that stuff, right?" I throw my hands in the air.

"I don't know," Elijah answers. "Jigger, jig, jig, I talked to him about it a lot the other day when he gave me that long apology, but I didn't really understand it any better at the end of his apology than I did at the beginning." He shrugs. "I guess it's something between him and Scott. Maybe none of us will ever understand unless we've been there. I felt bad for him, so I invited him to the pre-release, jigger, jig, jig. I hope you don't mind. I think he's probably a lot more like us than I originally thought. Maybe beneath the social roles we play, we're pretty much the same. What if that's the lesson of this whole book?"

I pretend to take his temperature with the back of my hand. "The delirium of editing must be getting to you. Isn't that the whole premise of the book?"

"Yeah, but —" he interjects.

"*Everybody* pretends to be something they're not to impress someone else because nobody feels comfortable in their own skin. Everything about today's modern social media is just like everyone walking around with a proverbial suit of no clothes." I punctuate my points with wild hand gestures.

He nods. "Jigger, jig, jig, I know that's what we set out to do, but having a goal to do something and then having it play out in front of us are two different things."

"Yeah, I know what you mean. I thought it would feel one way when I rehearsed it in my head. Even watching everything that was normal crumble in front of me, it was weird. I didn't get the feeling of vindication and power I thought I would at seeing the formerly popular kids struggle with not being the ones on the top. Honestly, it was entertaining for a while, but it turned out to suck to see other people getting hurt. I didn't want anyone to feel what I went through, even if it was my former tormentors. I felt more than a little weird and uncomfortable. Do you think it feels as weird to them too, or are we the only ones who notice the difference?"

"I don't know. Jigger, jig, jig, I guess we'll figure it all out on the day of the launch, won't we?" Elijah replies with a lopsided grin.

"I still can't believe you wrote it that way." I shake my head. "I'm not sure the line between art and life and life imitating art has ever been so thin."

Chapter Ten

Elijah

Because I've had Tourette's syndrome, for basically as long as I can remember, I've been in a lot of nerve-racking situations. Usually, I avoid being center stage, but being friends with Sadie has allowed me to spread my wings a little.

She still hangs out with a bunch of her friends from the School for the Deaf, and several of them give the word 'outgoing' a brand-new meaning. It's impossible to be shy around them. The standing joke is that no one cares about my verbal tics because they can all turn off their hearing aids or cochlear implants and ignore me. Surprisingly, even though I'm so nervous I've chewed a pack and a half of gum this morning, I'm not a tic-machine yet.

Heather, the owner of Joy and Tiers, walks up and asks quietly, "Are we all set, Elijah?"

"Jigger, jig, jig, I'm about as ready as I'll ever be. This isn't insane, right?"

"I think it's brilliant. I know how you feel though. I was the same way when I opened the bakery. Just so you know,

I had to talk my husband and his friends out of wearing their full military fatigues. They wanted to add a bit of realism to the evening."

"Although it would've been funny, I want everyone to make their choice freely, without coercion of any sort," I say with an anxious grin.

It's interesting how my goals for this book changed along the way. Initially, Sadie and I started this novel as a simple exercise in spoofing the culture of popularity. We started by studying what it takes to make a story or a meme go viral, and we wondered if there's a parallel in what makes a group of kids popular. Yet, the more we played with that dynamic, the more clear it became that popularity, and the lack of it, is a much more complex issue.

Finally, Sadie and I decided maybe it wasn't right for only us to determine the outcome of the book. We wrote and illustrated two endings. One isn't even completely written yet. Sadie and I won't be in charge of choosing which one will be published in the book — our fellow students will be. We figured it was only fair, since for several months, they've been the unwitting inspiration for most of our characters.

Without the involvement of our classmates, this book would've been much more difficult to write. Although our decision is about to give Mrs. Gable an apoplexy, we're giving our fellow students the final say.

I look over at Sadie, hunched over Gabriel's computer. They're still trying to work out a few technical glitches with her illustrations. He's been teaching her a computer program which allows her to take pictures of her artwork and draw over them on a large electronic tablet, as if it's a canvas, and convert the drawing into a computer file for publication.

It's been interesting to watch her during this process. Everything usually comes breathlessly easy for Sadie, but this has had a steep learning curve and it has been a real challenge for her. It's the first time I've ever seen her frustrated about anything other than people being rude to me. However, she finally seems to be getting the hang of it. Apparently, based on the deep frown, she and Gabriel must have encountered some last-minute software glitch. Her brows are furrowed as her fingers fly across the tablet and she discusses something hotly with Gabriel. He has a search engine up on his own computer. Finally, they both smile and relax against the backs of their chairs as they high-five each other.

Sadie looks stunning. It's almost as if she's morphed into Anderson Fischer. She's wearing a tailored business suit and high heels with a silky shirt and pearls. She even has glasses like the avatar. If I'm honest with myself, you'd be hard pressed to recognize me as the student I was at the beginning of the year either. I carry myself with much more confidence — I suppose you could call it swagger. I stand straighter and look people in the eye now.

I noticed the most dramatic difference in my life in the crowded hallways between classes first. Every day, dozens of times a day, there are small power exchanges where people determine your social status by your right to travel in the hall. As I became half of Anderson Fischer, and that entity began to mean something, I became less willing to give up my personal space to others. In turn, people asked me to do it less. With very few exceptions, Sadie and I are rarely cornered and picked on now.

My dad asked me the other day what I thought was different. I told him I didn't really know. It's not as if I haven't always been a writer. It's not as if I haven't gone to school with most of these kids before. I don't even think it's the fact that I'm in high school now.

If I'm honest with myself, it's because Sadie gave me the courage to believe I was worth more than other people's expectations of me.

It's time for me to prove her rock-solid trust has been well placed.

CHAPTER ELEVEN

SADIE

I have a ton riding on tonight, but I don't think I have as much at stake as Elijah. As he fiddles with his tie, it's obvious he's incredibly stressed out; but he's got this covered. There isn't an outcome which could happen tonight he's not prepared for. Elijah's my best friend, but put quite simply, he's a genius. Even though the school faculty is nervous about today, I'm really not. I've learned so much about my new classmates, I actually have faith that most of them are here for the right reasons today.

I may be proven radically wrong — most days you can stamp gullible across my forehead. But, I want to believe not everybody in the world is as shallow as social media and television portray us to be. I guess today will be an interesting test of my theory. I can't really tell which way Elijah thinks it's going or how he hopes it will go. Unfortunately, we won't have a front row seat, at least not live. Heather's husband, Tyler, and his ex-army buddy,

Trevor, set up surveillance cameras so we can watch what happens, but in order to not inadvertently influence the process, we won't be present during the first stage.

"Is everybody in place?" Heather's sister, Madison, the investigative reporter, asks.

Everyone at the entrances taking tickets nods as they speak into little earpieces.

I squeeze Elijah's hand, and we step into the screening room backstage. "Good luck. It's been a blast being your study buddy, but it's been even more fun to be your friend."

Over the next hour or so, I watch with Madison's husband, Trevor, as people line up. Initially, we had sorted the lines into some priority but later decided it might be better if they were random. We held an additional lottery at the school and gave out another two hundred and fifty tickets.

I'm watching lines A and B, and Elijah is watching lines C and D. We're not exactly sure how many of the five hundred we invited will bother to show up. Aside from the second lottery we held, we didn't publicize the event on campus. We only used social media.

The instructions given to the ticket takers were simply to ask, "Good evening, who are you here to see today?" If they answer Anderson Fischer, the guest will be escorted to an auditorium. However, if they answer Aidan O'Brien, they'll be instructed that the concert was overbooked, and there are only seats left in the overflow room. Those who choose to stay only for the concert will be escorted to a different room and later dismissed.

As I watch the sorting process, many of the choices don't surprise me. Most of our friends choose Anderson

Fischer and are escorted to the auditorium. I am a little surprised to see several people who, at the beginning of the year, we would've classified as not our biggest fans, be included in the group who came specifically to see us. There were a few people which answered both. We decided to give them the benefit of the doubt and put them in the auditorium.

At the end of the selection process, the ratio was better than I expected it to be, considering there was a last-minute surge in the Aidan O'Brien fans. On closer inspection, many of those didn't have the hand-drawn tickets Tara and I made for them. They downloaded a JPEG from the Internet and were trying to get in with "scalped" tickets. I'm not sure whether to be flattered or insulted. Since most of those ticket holders had chosen Aidan, it didn't actually impact our results much, because the next step is the critical one.

After everyone is seated, I adopt my Anderson Fischer persona and go out on stage to introduce the book. I go through my introductory remarks and explain how I illustrated the book in collaboration with Elijah. On cue, Tyler shuts down my Power Point presentation, and the crowd grows restless.

Someone from the back of the room shouts, "I thought Aidan O'Brien was coming."

Elijah comes out on stage and whispers in my ear. "Jigger, jig, jig, I hope you have good health insurance, because they'll eat you alive."

I stifle a grin as I turn to the audience and somberly announce, "I'm so sorry. Mr. O'Brien has been detained at the airport due to a security scare. He's not sure he'll be able to make it tonight. He deeply apologizes."

A voice from the side of the auditorium shouts, "See? I told you it was all a hoax. Jigger-nut probably doesn't even know Aidan O'Brien and lied to us all along. Let's get outta here."

I'm trying very hard not to look at Tara as she interprets for me. The members of the audience don't know we all went on a three-hour hike last weekend for Elijah's birthday, and Aidan surprised him with a new set of rock climbing shoes.

Keeping my face as neutral as possible, I respond, "Anyone who wants to leave is more than welcome to. If you're not here for *Behind Glass Bars*, you're likely to find the next couple of hours pretty boring anyway."

In the first row, I can read the lips of a group of girls chattering to each other. "I told you that you can't believe what you read on the Internet. This was bogus."

The other girl responds, "No, my stepbrother's cousin goes to this school. He says this is a real project."

"You're so lame. Who would want to go to a meeting about a book? We're just here for Aidan O'Brien. Come on, let's get out of here."

"Actually, I am the kind of person who wants to stay for a meeting about a book. I don't care who else is coming," she says defiantly.

A bunch of my friends are sitting around her and can see Tara interpret her conversation. They applaud and cheer for her. Eventually, her friends decide to ditch her. My friend Zach offers them a ride home, much to the delight of everyone in the auditorium.

After the commotion settles down, I address the crowd again. "Does anyone else want to leave?"

I survey the crowd, but clearly the mood has changed, and everyone shakes their head.

Elijah steps out onto the stage and messes with the mic before saying in a halting voice, "Hello, I'm Elijah Fischer – the other half of Anderson Fischer, jigger, jig, jig. Honestly, if it weren't for Sadie Anderson, there wouldn't even be an Anderson Fischer, but she was brave enough to step forward and be my friend on her first day of school here, and it helps that she's probably the smartest person I've ever met. Jigger, jig, jig, those of you who have tickets issued by us have seen firsthand how talented Sadie is, and I would advise you to keep your ticket, because someday it will be worth some serious money."

A wave of soft laughter courses through the audience, but I notice several people pull their tickets out of their pockets and look at them a little more closely.

"Most of you have known me for a long time. Jigger, jig, jig, for those of you who don't, I have Tourette's syndrome. I won't even pretend that it doesn't make me do weird stuff. It does. The more I try to stop it from making me do strange things, the more likely I am to pop out with weird phrases like jigger."

I can hear a few awkward snickers and whispers, but Elijah presses ahead, "It could be worse. I have friends who are way more prone to use some vile cuss words."

Someone from the audience yells, "I have a friend who does that. It's pretty funny in church."

Elijah raises an eyebrow. "Probably not for him." I look back out at the audience as he continues his answer,

"Sometimes I randomly hit or scratch myself or have involuntary muscle twitches called tics. For some reason, Tourette's often occurs with obsessive-compulsive disorder, so I can get focused on counting things like the strokes of a pencil when I'm writing or how many times I brush my teeth or tie my shoes, jigger, jig, jig. Trust me, it's as frustrating for me to deal with as it is for you to listen to."

Elijah backs off into the shadows of the stage and motions for me to take over.

I step up to the podium and start the slideshow. "Now that we've got all the formalities out of the way, let's talk about *Behind Glass Bars*." I pivot, rescuing a very stressed Elijah. "Many of you might be thinking to yourselves, 'They just told us Aidan O'Brien probably isn't coming, and they gave us a brief little overview of the book and introduced themselves, so why are we still here?' I'll be happy to clear that up for you — or at least I'll try."

Several members of the audience shift uncomfortably in their seats, and for the first time tonight, I start to get very uncomfortable. The weight of my announcement is almost unbearable, but I have to press on. "Like any other authors, Elijah and I are influenced by the world around us, but in this case, we were even more influenced than most. We wanted to write a book about the impact of social media on young people and how it has changed our perceptions about ourselves."

"We looked around the Internet and reality television, and we noticed there were a number of people who were famous just for being on social media ... and we wondered if we could replicate that and study the impact on people around us. In the end, the story became something for you and about you. Elijah and I decided to allow you to have the last word about how the story ends."

Tara interprets a question from one of my friends. "What does that mean exactly?" Jasmine signs as she flips a bright blue dreadlock over her shoulder.

"It means you guys have a choice. I don't want to ruin the story for all of you, but in *Behind Glass Bars,* Elijah and I created a fantastical utopian world — perfect until the inhabitants started to compete against each other and invented lying. Initially, lying seemed like a way to get ahead. Eventually, they discovered that each lie they told created a fine strand of glass, which creates a cage. At first, that was going to be the whole point of our modern-day fairytale, but as we studied the impact of social media on popularity, we realized there really isn't any perfect side to be on in this equation. Elijah has a perfectly satisfactory ending written for this book that would please most reviewers."

Before I can go further, I'm interrupted by a loud voice from the middle of the room. "What's the other option?"

"Well, this one's going to take a little work. We'd like to use what we learned over the last few months to change and redraft the story to show that it might be possible to create a fair social environment for everyone. Elijah would like to talk to all of you individually about how the changes over the past few months have impacted you personally. This is going to require some time and brutal honesty. It's not easy to bare your soul to this process, and some of you might not want to do this, so majority wins here." I walk to the edge of the stage and look into the audience. "If you have a ticket, hold it up in the air if you want to do the simple straightforward approach."

The girl with dark hair from the front row speaks up. "What if I don't have a legitimate ticket, but I really want one?"

"I suppose if you're passionate enough about books to sit through this whole thing, I can fix that. Anybody got paper?"

Ms. Gable tears a piece of paper off her legal pad and hands it to me along with her pen. It's a little ballpoint pen, and not what I'm used to drawing with, but it'll work. I quickly sketch the girl who I learn is named Maisie. It turns out she's from the same school as Gabriel. I look up at the audience and ask if there's anyone else who needs a ticket. Much to my surprise, about seven people step forward. It seems they heard Aidan O'Brien was going to appear in concert on Twitter, but they were also book fans and decided to stay once they were told he wouldn't be here.

After I issue tickets to everyone, I call for a vote. "Interviews it is. Ready for a re-write, Elijah?"

I glance over at Elijah, and he appears deathly pale as he turns to Mrs. Gable. "Jigger, jig, jig, is it too late to change the publication date to next year?"

Mrs. Gable laughs. "It's already in the works."

"Good, jigger, jigger, jigger jig, jigger, I thought I would only have a month and a half to do all these interviews." Elijah turns to me. "I guess the good thing is that you and I are only freshmen. We've got plenty of time until we graduate."

Cody Davis shoots his arm up in the air. "So what

you're saying is that this whole book is just an elaborate joke on all your friends? That doesn't seem very fair."

"Initially, we planned to have this be a more lighthearted satire piece on the effect of social media on popularity. You know, a spoof on *The Emperor's New Clothes*, but we ended up learning so much about ourselves and everyone else around us that it became far bigger than a parody of our Kim Kardashian, Facebook, Snapchat, my-life-can-be-summed-up-in-a-filtered-pic world. I'm sorry if you feel like we took advantage of you. That was never our intention." I try to explain, but it's difficult to convey the metamorphosis that Elijah and I went through over the course of the year.

Cody turns to the crowd. "What do you wanna bet I'm an ugly, jerk-face of a villain in this book?"

I smile at him. "I think you'll probably be surprised."

I look out at the auditorium full of faces and ask, "Any more questions about Behind Glass Bars?"

From behind me, I hear a voice respond, "No, but I have another question … Who's ready to have a good time?"

The crowd gasps as Aidan walks on stage, clipping his guitar strap on. He shakes Elijah's hand as he says, "Sorry I'm late, but thanks for keeping everybody occupied for me. Something tells me they were more interested in what you guys have been saying than anything I could sing tonight." Aidan pulls the microphone off the podium and puts it on a mic stand as he says, "Ladies and gentlemen, pay attention to Anderson Fischer. I believe they're the next great team in fiction."

CHAPTER TWELVE

ELIJAH

Slapping the menu down on the cheesy red vinyl tablecloth with a garish black dragon in the middle, I look across the table at Cody. "Jigger, jigger, jig why this place? I'm jigger a little afraid to order. Jigger, it looks pretty dicey."

Cody glances around the restaurant with its stereotypical decorations which look like they're from the nineteen seventies and shrugs. "I know it doesn't look like much. But the food here is actually pretty good. I like it. Besides, Scott wouldn't be caught dead in here. He is allergic to shrimp and is convinced that people are out to get him and might actually poison him. So, he doesn't eat here — like ever. We can have a private conversation here."

"Jigger, okay," I respond skeptically. "I didn't realize you were still avoiding Scott, jigger, jig, jig."

Cody nods. "Yeah, once Scott wasn't the most popular guy on campus he started acting like my little brother when he doesn't get his way."

"This was a newsflash, jigger, jig, jig?" I ask, not able to keep the sarcasm out of my voice.

"Right. I suppose that's how you saw him all along. But to me he was the guy I wanted to be. He was a popular athlete with girls hanging all over him and more friends than he knew what to do with."

I pin Cody with an intense gaze. "Jigger, jigger, jigger." I pause to take a drink of water. I don't even bother to try to hide my tic in front of Cody anymore. He's hung out with Sadie and me enough that if he's not used to it by now, tough bananas. I draw in a deep breath and try again. "Did Scotty really have that many friends or was everyone afraid of him?"

Cody takes a couple bites of egg drop soup before he answers, "I used to think we were all tight. But since I got kicked off the team for wrecking Sadie's stuff, I know better. Nobody gives a rat's butt about me if I can't score points on the team. I mean … I tried to get notes from my bio class, so I could study for the test. When I got suspended, my so-called friends wouldn't even walk across the street so I could make copies."

"You should've asked me. I'm in that class with you."

"Why would you care? I was messing with your girl."

"First of all, Sadie is not my girl. We're just friends. Let's just say this project taught me an awful lot about peer pressure, jigger, jig, jig. I decided there's a bunch I don't understand."

"Yeah, I'm discovering there's a crap load of stuff I don't get. I probably understand least about me. I know you don't believe me, but I don't usually act the way I did when I was around Scott. I've got little brothers and I don't treat them the way I treated you and whoever else Scott didn't like around campus. My dad would kill me if he knew the kind of person I was. I'm already grounded for life for being kicked off the team. My parents were counting on me getting a football scholarship. I don't know what I'm gonna do now."

When Sadie and I started Project Utopia, we meant it to be a satirical take on social media and the fairness of high school relationships. We never dreamed it would change the social dynamics within our school and affect people's lives. I swallow hard. "I'm sorry. Jigger, jig, jigger, jig, jig, jig … We just meant to make fun of reality TV and Facebook, we didn't mean to wreck your scholarship or anything."

Cody grimaces. "You and Sadie didn't do that. I did that to myself. I bought into Scott's hatred of anyone he thought was inferior to him and I let it rule my life — for years. I let him change who I am. Even months later, I can't figure out how I let that happen."

I shrug. "I'm not sure how that happens either. You can change. I have no clue how to fix the scholarship situation. I know that Aidan O'Brien runs all sorts of camps for youth. Some of them are at risk youth and some of them have disabilities like me and Sadie. He's always looking for peer counselors for them. Someone like you with athletic talent and good grades would be a natural fit."

Cody's jaw goes slack. It takes him a few moments to regain his composure. "Aidan O'Brien, as in mega-superstar, top of the charts, Grammy-winner? That dude?"

I nod. "Jigger … jig, yep. He's also a really great husband, pool player and all-around funny guy."

"What do I tell him about what I did?" Cody asks with a frown. "Never mind, he's probably read about it in the paper."

"I would recommend the truth. You probably don't know all of Aidan's story. But he's gone through some pretty rough times himself. He hasn't always made the smartest choices either. If anybody's going to understand, it's probably Aidan and Tara."

"I don't know. Getting kicked off the team and suspended from school is pretty bad," Cody argues. "Heck, the school doesn't even know half of the bad stuff I did. If they knew, I would've probably been expelled."

"Jigger, jig, jig, all I know is that you were big enough to apologize to Sadie and me. You've worked hard for your grades. If you want a chance to start over, this is probably as big a shot as you're gonna get. Now, you have to decide if you believe in yourself enough to take it."

Cody scowls at me. "Were you always this smart?"

"Pretty much," I answer.

"How come I never knew this?" Cody asks with a puzzled expression.

"I dunno. Maybe because you were too busy beating the snot out of me, jigger, jig, jig."

"I need start making better life choices."

I pick up Cody's phone and program a phone number in it. "You can start by calling Aidan."

Cody sighs. "All right, point taken. I suppose all of this is going to go in that book of yours. I guess I've earned the role of super villain."

"Jigger, jig, jigger, Cody, I'm here as your friend.

Nothing goes in the book without your permission. You might be surprised how I see you. Now that I know you a little better, I don't think you're truly a villain. I see you as a guy with hero tendencies who merely lost his way."

"Could you try to be a little less nice? I'm already feeling guilty enough for the years I treated you like crap," Cody rolls his eyes.

"Sorry, Dude." I smirk. "Jigger, jig, jig, I'm not letting you off the hook that easily. You should feel bad. You were a jerk for a whole decade."

"I know it doesn't make up for it, but lunch is on me."

I chuckle. "Jigger, jig, jig, well, it's a start. Make sure you call Aidan. I can't believe I'm saying this, but I'll put in a good word for you."

"I can't believe you're saying it either, but I guess it goes to show people really can change. Thanks, man."

Chapter Thirteen

Sadie

Paint drips on Cody's hand as his electric paint gun shakes as I fill it. "Cody relax. It's going to be fine. We are painting the side of the building — not the Sistine Chapel. Besides, you're just helping me with the color blocking. Jasmine and I will go back in with airbrushes and do the fine detail work. This is supposed to be fun."

"That's easy for you to say. You guys are actually artists. I'm just the dumb jock. I can barely help my little brothers do paint by numbers."

"You forget I know better. I saw the map you did for geology class. That was some pretty nice detailed work and shading. Under all your bluster, there is an artist hidden there somewhere. Don't worry about it, if you mess up, we can fix it. But I don't think you can mess up. I think you can have fun. Besides, this is art it's open for interpretation. We're just putting the Scooby-Doo van and the clown car on the side of the new art studio. It's not exactly precision work."

Cody looks stricken. "I'm trying to make a good impression on Aidan. I want him to give me a job since I

"

messed up my chances for a scholarship."

Jasmine comes over and stands beside me as she pulls her bright blue and purple dreadlocks up and puts them in a ponytail. "Oh, I wouldn't worry about that. I think you took care of that last weekend when you picked up Jena Saunders and carried her on the rest of our nature hike after the wheel broke on her wheelchair; not everyone would've done that."

Cody shrugs. "She didn't want to be left behind while everybody had fun. It was the only decent thing to do."

"Exactly. It's what a good guy does. You're not your past. I think Aidan totally gets that. I know I was impressed." I screw on the lid to his pressure painter and give it back to him. "There is a piece of plywood over there we been practicing on if you want to try a few strokes."

"Hey … Sadie. I'm sorry I destroyed your stuff. I just want to say that."

I reach over and put my arm around his waist. "I know Cody. You've said that before. I accept your apology."

"At first, I was just sorry you figured out it was me. Now that I understand what project utopia meant to you and how personal those drawings were to you guys, I really am sorry I destroyed your vision."

"Thanks Cody. I appreciate it. I'm glad you understand now." I squeeze his waist In a sideways hug. "Everywhere I need you to paint in that color I marked with a big Y. When you're ready to change colors, come get me. I'll be working on the computer with Gabriel. Jasmine will be working with you coming behind you with a smaller airbrush. If you have any questions about the design, you can ask her."

"Are you sure you trust me with this?"

"Sure, that's the funny thing about life. Mistakes can be fixed.

———•———

I slide a soda under Gabriel's nose as he watches screens flashed by on my computer. "Were you able to get the updates to install on my computer?"

"Finally. Did you know you had two different virus protection programs running that conflicted with each other. It's a wonder your computer even worked."

I roll my eyes. "You can thank my dad for that little development. He can't pass up a free trial of software of any type. It doesn't matter how many times I warn him."

"Lovely. Anyway, I think I've got it fixed. We should be able to upload your final pictures so you guys can put your book up for pre-release if you're ready."

"I'm ready. I only have two drawings I want to switch out. I don't know where Elijah is. I think the only interview he has left to complete is the one with Cody. I'm not really sure how he plans to wrap that chapter up. I don't know if even he has figured that out."

Gabriel arches his eyebrow at me. He looks out the window at where Cody is painting the side of the building and Jasmine is pointing at another portion of the wall. "What do you make of him? Do you think he's playing us all? Do you think his sudden transformation is real?"

"I might be gullible, but I think his transformation is real. I'm not so sure he was ever a hard-core believer in the hate Scott preached. I think Cory has the same problem all the rest of us have. I believe he just did what he had to do to survive and fit in. I don't think he understood what it was like to be us until he fell from grace with Scott and the shoe was suddenly on the other foot — as the saying goes."

Gabriel shakes his head and glares toward the window where Cody was just standing. "I'm not sure I buy that. I'm sorry, I've been on the receiving end of so much hate. To me, this guy is like the racist jerks who have picked on me my whole life. I just wonder if he's really changed all that much."

I sigh. "I don't really know. Elijah seems to believe he has. He knows them better than I do since they grew up together. Aidan is willing to give him another chance. His apology seemed pretty legit to me so, I guess I'll just wait and see."

"Speaking of reinventing yourself, are you and Elijah ready to become Anderson Fisher? You know, my Aunt Madison wants to interview you guys for her television show once you guys publish your book, right?"

"She does? Why would she want to talk to us? I thought she did investigative reporting."

Gabriel types some information into his computer and pulls up the website about her television show. "See she has a new television show that covers all sorts of stuff. When I went over to Grandma and Grandpa's for dinner, I was talking to her about helping you with your project and she thought it would be cool if you went on her television show. She said you could even sign if you wanted to help reach a broader audience."

I grin. "I think that would be really cool. I'm not sure how Elijah would feel though. Thanks for watching out for me."

Gabriel looks embarrassed. "Thanks, don't mention it. That's what friends do for each other." He gazes out the window.

He points at Cody. "I suppose you should probably go rescue your other friend. He's looking a little overwhelmed by the paint gun. Then again, it might not be the paint gun at all. Jasmine seems to have him running in circles."

I laugh. "She seems to have that effect on a lot of people."

EPILOGUE

ELIJAH

I CAN'T BELIEVE IT'S been a whole year. Actually, it's been fifty-three weeks but, who's counting? If you would've asked me two years ago if I thought I would ever be waiting for a book I co-wrote to appear on the New York Times bestseller list, I would've said you're as crazy as I am odd. Yet, that's what I'm doing.

I pull up Sadie's number and hit send. Perhaps I should pay more attention to the real world because it's not even seven on a Saturday morning. When I notice, I decide to hang up, but I'm too late.

Her voice is groggy with sleep. "EF, do you realize what time it is? Gabriel and I aren't picking you guys up until four o'clock this afternoon. When is a girl supposed to get her beauty rest? This better be important."

"I think today might actually be *the day*," I announce, excitement making my voice squeak weirdly.

"The day for what? I thought you and Maisie were just going to the prom as friends."

"We are!" I exclaim. "That's not even what I'm talking about. Put your Anderson Fischer hat on. I'm talking about the book. Our numbers have been great this week. We'll probably make one of the lists this morning. The weird thing is, I'm not sure which list. We might make fantasy, or we might make it on to the memoir list."

"Congratulations, Elijah! I'm so excited for you. Still, if I've learned one thing during this process, it's that it doesn't really matter whether we ever make those lists or any other."

I sputter. "Wha-what do you mean it doesn't matter? This is the freakin' *New York Times Bestseller List*, and we did this whole thing so you would have something to put into your college portfolio, remember?"

"Exactly! I do have something beautiful to put in my college portfolio. In fact, I have the best book I've ever read to put in there, thanks to you. With or without the endorsement of the *NYT Bestseller List*, I have something that I'm so proud to put in front of every college I apply to. Look at us! We're going to prom at a different school because we have the confidence to believe in ourselves enough and put ourselves out there. When we started, I was afraid if you knew me, you wouldn't like me, but now I know differently. If a college or a bestseller list can't figure out how amazing we are, we'll move to the next one."

I laugh at my best friend's logic — but she's right. Even though we can't pick and choose bestsellers lists, we can choose how much they impact our lives. "You make a good point, 'Oh Wise One.' Now, are you sure I really have to wear a tux to this thing tonight?"

The last thing I hear before Sadie hangs up is a strangled groan of frustration and a vague threat to cut up all my hoodies if I show up in anything less than tails.

I'm incredibly lucky. On one of the worst days of my academic career I found a best friend who saw the real me and decided she liked me anyway. Life doesn't get better than that.

I close my computer and turn on a random soccer game on television. Sadie's right. As cool as outside recognition is, it doesn't measure up to the knowledge that I know my writing changed lives — especially my own.

———◆———

Sadie and Gabriel are cracking up over something a bunch of kids are doing over in the photo booth area.

Maisie rolls her eyes. "What do you want to bet The Fearsome Seven will make the front page of the student newspaper again this week?"

Gabriel nods. "They'll probably have another feature page in the yearbook too." He turns to me and explains, "They're like the definition of popular in this school."

I shrug. "Jigger, jig, jigger, popularity isn't necessarily what it seems. They could be really lonely under all those jokes and smiles."

Maisie looks surprised. "Really? They always look like they're having so much fun."

"Yeah," Sadie confirms. "That was the thing we found over and over when we talked to people. It wasn't just about the front they put on for social media. A lot of people were pretending for their friends too."

Maisie's eyes widen. "It's true though. Once my friends figured out how much I really like books and dislike just hanging around shopping, we kinda drifted apart. I wasn't willing to pretend to be somebody else anymore."

"Oh, Geez! I'm sorry Project Utopia made things more awkward for you. That was never our intent," I say as I flinch.

Maisie lays her hand on my shoulder and I jump. "Relax! I like you. You guys are much more fun to hang around. At least now, I don't feel like my brain cells are at risk of imploding from lack of use."

I shift uncomfortably on the hard plastic chair. "Jigger, jig, jigger, Thank you, I guess. Are you thirsty? Can I get you some punch?"

Maisie grins at me. "Thank you, but no. I promised my mom I wouldn't drink the punch. Apparently, she had an unfortunate experience with the punch at her high school prom. I promised her I wouldn't drink anything except water."

"Understood. I'll get you a bottle of water. I know where the vending machine is. I saw it on the way in. I'll be right back." I'm so nervous I practically sprint into the hallway.

As I round the corner to the hallway with the vending machines, I come face-to-face with a very startled Mindy. I haven't seen her since the day we launched the Utopian Fine Arts Society. She draws in a startled breath before she asks, "Elijah? What are you doing here? I thought you went to school with Sadie."

"Umm ... I do. Jigger, jig, jig Sadie is your cousin Gabriel's date and I came with Maisie. Why are you here?

Aren't you a little young to come to high school dance?"

Mindy looks crestfallen. "To go to the dance? Yes. To perform? I guess I have permission. I am playing with Tasha. She was on a TV show once with Uncle Aidan. I play the acoustic guitar and do backup vocals for her. I don't usually do gigs this big, but Stella is sick."

"Is Aidan going to sing tonight?" I ask hopefully.

Mindy giggles. "Can you imagine the chaos it would cause if Uncle Aidan showed up? This school would be overrun. We are just here as a favor to Gabriel because he's on the student council. They wanted a good turnout to this dance so they could raise some funds for their senior trip next year. So, I guess you're stuck with me."

"Jigger, jig jigger, jig, jig, I'm embarrassed I didn't even know you sang"

Mindy winks. "I have lots of talents people don't know about. I need to get going so I can get ready to go on stage — but I will sing you and Maisie a song so you can slow dance together."

I take a moment to study Mindy. She has a very cool sophisticated Taylor Swift kind of vibe. I'll be looking forward to hearing her sing and it won't be just because I get to dance with Maisie.

As Mindy walks away with her guitar case slung over her shoulder she looks back at me. "By the way, I read your book. It's one of the coolest books I've ever read. Thanks for writing it. I'm not just saying that because I know you — I swear."

"That's probably the nicest thing anyone's ever said to me."

"Just so you know, lots of people will be saying things like that really soon. Get used to it."

Embarrassed, I fiddle with the vending machine and purchase a bottle of water for Maisie and rush back to my seat. When I get there I blurt to Maisie, "You'll never guess who I saw in the hall!"

Maisie's eyes light up with excitement. "Did you get to see Tasha Keeley? I heard she was coming."

I shake my head. "No, but she is here. I ran into Gabriel's cousin Mindy. She's going to sing you a song so we can dance."

The corner of Gabriel's mouth hitches up. "Wow! I bet you just made her whole night. She's been talking about you non-stop since she read *Behind Glass Bars*. She is a huge fan."

I flushed bright red. "You mean she wasn't making all that up just to be nice? Jig, jigger, jig."

Gabriel chuckles. "No … it's safe to say my cousin is one of your biggest fans. Something tells me the two of you have a lot in common."

THE END

The Hidden Beauty Series continues in Jude's Song where you can read more about Tasha Keeley and Mindy Whitaker.

Elijah's story continues in Tempting Fate.

NOTE FROM THE AUTHOR

Dear Reader,

Thanks for giving this little novella a read. If you liked reading about people who are not so stereotypical, then I've got good news…

…there's more.

The Hidden Beauty Series continues in Jude's Song

What if the way the world sees you is not the way you see yourself?

Once former competitors, Aidan O'Brien offered Tasha Keeley the record deal of a lifetime.

There's only one problem. Tasha isn't sure she wants it.

She has different plans.

For as long as she can remember, Tasha has been on stage performing. Now she wants to leave and become the person she always dreamed of being.

Jude Hernandez thinks Tasha is crazy.

He'd give anything to trade places. He's worked his whole life for an opportunity like that.

Can Jude and Tasha see eye to eye and conquer challenges together while making beautiful music?

You'll love this sweet interracial romance with a hint of danger.

Get Jude's Song now in paperback, e-book version or through Kindle Unlimited now.

Thank you,

~Mary

Because love matters, differences don't.

ACKNOWLEDGEMENTS

I'd like to acknowledge all of the individuals with disabilities I've worked with in the past, who've given me enormous amounts of inspiration about overcoming incredible obstacles while maintaining good humor and grace. I would specifically like to recognize Emily Holmes for her advocacy in the field of Tourette's Syndrome acceptance. She taught me so much–I hope I've represented it well.

A special thank you to Erika Van Eck for bringing the original team together which inspired the anthology in which this story originally appeared. The fight against bullying is ongoing. Kudos to my beautiful team of supporters for making it possible for me to participate.

A big shout out to the stunning photography of James Garner and my beautiful cover model, Paige. You brought Sadie to life in the most magnificently, realistic way possible. I am forever grateful for your artistry.

Just a personal note to everyone who bullied me: Thank you — but I win.

About the Author

I have been lucky enough to live my own version of a romance novel. I married the guy who kissed me at summer camp. He told me on the night we met that he was going to marry me and be the father of my children.

Eventually, I stopped giggling when he said it, and we've been married for over thirty years. We have two children. The oldest is a Doctor of Osteopathy. He is across the United States completing his residency, but when he's done, he is going to come back to Oregon and practice Family Medicine. Our youngest son is now tackling high school where he is an honor student. He is interested in becoming an EMT.

I write full time now. I have published more than thirty books and have several more underway. I volunteer my time to a variety of causes. I have worked as a Civil Rights Attorney and diversity advocate. I spent several years working for various social service agencies before becoming an attorney.

In my spare time, I love to cook, decorate cakes and, of course, I obsessively, compulsively read.

I would be honored if you would take a few moments out of your busy day to check out my website,

MaryCrawfordAuthor.com. While you're there, you can sign up for my newsletter and get a free book. I will be announcing my upcoming books and giving sneak peeks as well as sponsoring giveaways and giving you information about other interesting events.

If you have questions or comments, please E-mail me at Mary@MaryCrawfordAuthor.com or find me on the following social networks:

Facebook: www.facebook.com/authormarycrawford

Website: MaryCrawfordAuthor.com

Twitter: www.twitter.com/MaryCrawfordAut